Taken by Two Lifeguards

Taken, Volume 11

Jasmine Black

Published by Spunky Girl Publishing, 2022.

Also by Jasmine Black

Taken by Two Elves

Standalone
Shared Boxed Set

Taken by Two Lifeguards

Twenty-two-year-old professional swimmer and Olympic hopeful, Katie White, goes to the beach every day to continue work on her training by swimming in the ocean...and to do some secret naughty stuff on the side.

She also loves the lifeguard eye candy. Skimpy swim trunks on tanned muscular bodies put her in a really good mood. But the lifeguards don't seem to know she exists, especially after she broke up with her lifeguard boyfriend, Chad.

When Katie suddenly gets caught in a malicious storm, two lifeguards come to her rescue. One of them is Chad!

Stranded in the first-aid shack and being almost dead has made Katie awfully cold and her two lifeguard rescuers are going to warm Katie up nice and slow...

Other stories by Jasmine Black include:

Taken by Two Doctors, Taken by Three Doctors, Taken by Two Bikers, Taken by Three Bikers, Taken by Two Billionaires, Taken by Three Billionaires, Taken by Two Bosses, Taken by Two Cowboys, Taken by Three Cowboys, Taken by Two Firefighters, Taken by Two Carpenters, Taken by Two Personal Trainers, Taken by Two Santas, Taken by Two Elves, Taken by Three Bodyguards, Taken by Two Cops, Taken by Two Prison Guards, Taken by Two Lifeguards, Taken by Two Mountain Men and more!

Copyright

Author Note

This is a work of fiction. Characters, places, settings, and events presented in this book are purely of the author's imagination and bear no resemblance to any actual person, living or dead or to any actual events, places, and/or settings.

Chapter One

I'm always pretty tired after putting in a full day of swim training at the local gym, but I force myself to come to the beach every day just so I can relax and have some naughty private time. I've been professionally training as a swimmer for the Olympics since I was ten and I've rarely seen a sunrise unless the pool I'm training in has windows. My coach insists if I keep up with the weights, the workouts, yoga, hypoxic training and a bunch of other stuff, she will make sure I win gold at the next Olympics. She's been saying that since I can remember.

I'm twenty-two now and I've been close to winning on a few occasions but I'm getting older and I'm not so hopeful of winning gold anymore.

I've slowly come to realize that swimming professionally and winning competitions is not my vision. Instead, it is my grandmother's dream *for* me or more precisely, her dream for herself. She hadn't been able to achieve it because she'd been forced to marry at sixteen. She'd gotten pregnant and to avoid a family scandal, her parents had pushed her to marry the guy who'd knocked her up. A few months later, my dad was born.

My grandmother has been my primary caretaker since I was nine. That's when my parents died in a car crash. I've been swimming since then, to please her.

Grandpa died suddenly a few years ago of a massive heart attack and I've continued to live with her because I can't afford living elsewhere while I train, so I take care of her when I'm at home.

Lately though, I've been looking for every excuse under the sun not to go home. I just feel trapped; feeding her mashed up food and emptying her commode when her arthritis acts up and she can't care for herself just isn't a life goal for me. She has a bad habit of guilt tripping me into caring for her, saying that she took care of my sorry ass for many years and now it's my turn to give back.

The highlight of my day is coming here to the beach to get away from everything.

The lifeguard eye candy is a bonus. Hot, tanned muscles on very tall, lean men wearing skimpy swim trunks make my pulse and pussy react. For the longest time, those handsome hunks had been off limits for a shy girl like me, but one of them had asked me out earlier this summer and I'd said yes.

We were together for awhile, but we aren't anymore. He works here as a lifeguard and no other guy has asked me out since our breakup.

I also love the scenic short drive along the California coastline to get here. The hills are filled with expensive mansions on one side of the highway and on the other side there's white sandy beaches and dark blue ocean. For the longest time, I thought when I made it big at the Olympics I would buy one of those big houses. It would be better than living in that rat trap, one bedroom apartment with grandma.

But now I'm thinking of quitting grandma's dream and getting a good paying job, moving out and just figuring out what to do with the rest of my life. For sure, I'd still come here to the beach.

The sight of those hunky lifeguards sitting on their perches, their big muscles tense and their bodies fully alert and ready to tackle a potential drowning, always gets me into a mood to masturbate. That's another reason I come here, so I can swim out to the unmanned lighthouse miles down the coast and spend some quality time with myself.

I parked my car in the almost empty parking lot and wondered where everyone was today. As usual the late summer sun was bright, not a cloud in the sky and yet there was just a handful of vehicles nearby. I liked it better with lots of people. It gave me the opportunity to become a wallflower and just disappear into the ocean without one of the lifeguards watching me.

Oh well, I'd just stick to my routine.

I stuffed my wallet into the glove compartment, grabbed my towel, snapped my car key onto my necklace and got out of the car. The heat blasted against me like a furnace and I inhaled the salty air. I gazed along the beach, hoping my ex-boyfriend wasn't here today. It was awkward with him around, especially in the way things had ended between us.

I'd already changed into my swimsuit back at the gym, and I wore my white terrycloth robe and sandals as I strolled to the beach. There was one lifeguard perched on his lookout, but he was too far away for me to see who it might be and thankfully I was going the opposite way.

I was one of those shy young women who really didn't know how to talk to men. That's why I'd been surprised when Chad, a lifeguard, had taken an interest in me and we'd started dating.

But when I'd seen him and another lifeguard coming out of the first aid shack with one of those cute flirty blonde surfer girls who always hung around them, I knew *something* had been going on. I'd heard the rumors. Sometimes one or two or even three lifeguards would disappear in that shack for awhile with a female and the girl always came out with a big smile on her face.

Sometimes I wished I were one of those girls. But it was just a naughty fantasy that I toyed with in being with more than one guy at the same time. I was a good girl. Raised that way by my strict God-fearing grandmother. That's probably why my cheeks always went red when a guy talked to me. Even my ex, Chad, had commented on that issue.

Chad took night courses at the local college. He was going to be an electrician. It would be a decent job for him and I had thought he would be a good man for me. Oh well, I was twenty-two years old and I had no prospects of settling down with a guy that had future written all over him anyways, so why bother thinking about it.

In my opinion I wasn't Chad's equal in the take home pay department because I'd spent all my time training, instead of getting an education that would get me a well-paying job for my future.

Once again, I had my old fashion grandmother to blame, and of course, myself. Any winnings from competitions went back into the coach's salary and food and rent for us, instead of college courses. She expected me to marry some rich guy, but that wasn't going to happen because the last thing I wanted was to be dependant on a man for my shelter and food, like she'd been.

"Don't give away your milk, unless the farmer puts a ring on your finger," she'd say.

Damn hypocrite.

So, yeah, she thought I was still a virgin. But I wasn't. Tall, dark and dreamy Chad Samson had taken care of that on our second date and I'd loved it!

I found a secluded spot on the beach behind some high dunes and lay my towel down in the nice warm sand. Then I slipped off my sandals and robe and placed them neatly beside the towel. I wanted to portray the illusion that I was coming back soon. I removed my necklace with car key on it and slid it beneath the sand under the towel. I doubted anyone would even want to steal my old car that broke down every other week. They'd be doing me a favor if they did take it!

I walked toward the crashing breakers and noticed the surf was pretty rough with curling whitecaps. There were a string of screaming surfer girls catching the waves, but they didn't pay attention to me. Several of the lifeguard perches remained empty and I figured I knew where those guys were. In the first aid shack with one or two of those surfer girls.

What pleasures went on in that hut anyway? I'd be interested in finding out.

Maybe I shouldn't have freaked out on Chad after spying him coming out of there with another lifeguard and a girl several weeks ago.

When I told him I'd seen him, he'd gotten so pissed off saying if I'd have sex with him more often then he wouldn't have to look elsewhere. So, I'd told him to go right ahead and look elsewhere!

But I missed him. Missed his sweet smile and the twinkling of his brown eyes.

His endearing dream for me was for me to get out from under my grandmother's control.

The things I missed the most about him though, were his six pack abs, the gorgeous velvet-encased hard-as-a-rock mushroom-shaped cockhead that he'd taught me to take into my mouth and the forceful way his thick shaft made love to my quaking pussy, penetrating deep into my vagina until I was gasping from the fullness of his hard flesh and trembling from his scorching heat.

I blew out a tense breath as my pussy quivered with a need to be penetrated. I ran toward the roaring surf, trying to push Chad and my jealousy out of my mind.

Chapter Two

I jumped into the mild water, loving how it splashed forcefully against me.

Quickly, I walked further into the ocean until the water touched my hot, throbbing pussy.

The seductive back and forth caresses of the surf against my swollen clitoris had me gasping. I wished I could reach down and slip my fingers into my bikini bottom and rub my sensitive clit and make myself come. But I was out in the open. Someone could be watching.

I gazed up the beach where I could see my little target. The lighthouse perched on a spit, accessible only by water because they always kept the fifteen-foot-high chain link gate locked to prevent trespassers from hanging out there.

I held my breath and dove into the water, embracing the wet liquid engulfing my entire body. I swam underwater for as long as I could hold my breath before surfacing. The hot sun beat down on my head and face, but the rest of me was immersed in cool fluid.

I got into my synchronized swimming very quickly. My arms sliced through the water with ease, and I enjoyed getting the kinks out of my calf muscles by kicking my legs. I swam with my focus entirely on the lighthouse several miles away.

White waves curled around me trying to drag me under and salty water slapped against my face, pissing me off and yet I kept swimming. I was used to the challenges of the ocean. And the powerful roar of the surf crashing against the nearby beach empowered me.

I swam faster.

By the time I reached the sandy beach in front of the lighthouse, I felt invigorated, my body primed for some naughty alone time action.

Ocean water sluiced off my skin as I stepped onto the sunny beach. The hot sun pummelled my wet body and the scorching sand slipped between my tender toes while I walked around the base of the building. I knew the lighthouse was unmanned and after a quick exploration to confirm I was alone; I smiled and quickly removed my bikini top.

I gazed down the coastline to where I'd left my towel and sandals and noted the handful of people on the beach were the size of ants. I inhaled deeply and watched my breasts jiggle and jut with appreciation at being out and free. The hot sun pummelled my flesh and the wicked wind lapped at my nipples, caressing and arousing them until they were hard peaks.

Then I moved to the side of the lighthouse where I sat down on the soft bed of cool green moss that grew in the shade of the towering building and examined my pert breasts.

I like my breasts. They're not too big and not too small and they fit perfectly in Chad's palms. Sexual tension smoldered through me as I thought about him. He's six feet tall compared to my five feet five. And he has the softest lips. But maybe all guys had soft lips? I didn't know, as Chad was the only guy I'd ever kissed.

I inhaled deeply as I cupped my cool smooth mounds the way Chad used to do. He'd squeeze them gently, testing their weight and then his head would lower and he'd suck a nipple into his hot mouth, creating shivery sensations as he licked and nibbled.

Excitement roared through me as I pinched and pulled at my pink nipples whipping up an awesome throbbing pleasure pain that had me gasping at the intensity. Between my thighs I felt the warm cream of arousal seeping out of me.

Then I slipped out of my bikini briefs and lay on my back upon the soft moss. With one hand, I kept seductively smoothing my palm over my breasts, tweaking and pulling my nipples, relishing the pleasure which arrowed from my breasts to between my legs.

I lifted my knees and spread my legs, then slipped one hand between my thighs, moaning as my fingers found my hot engorged clitoris.

Slowly, softly, I began rubbing at the tight, sensitive bundle of nerves until pleasure quivered and more hot cream poured into my vagina.

Then I dipped a finger inside my channel, collecting my wetness, bringing out my cream and using it as lube as I massaged my tender clit.

I rubbed my clit harder, creating a yummy friction. Dipped my fingers between my soft labia folds and into my vagina to gather more hot cream. Then I massaged my swollen, wet clitoris harder and harder. Fiery need gripped me. I tweaked my nipples until they were solid pebbles and on fire with pleasure and pain.

My breath caught as tension consumed me. Sensitive nerve endings fired deep within and my pussy, my belly and my breasts tightened. My vagina clenched and I rapidly pistoned my finger into my channel like it was a mini-cock on a mission.

I rubbed my breasts until my body ached.

The orgasm neared, my breaths came faster and then my self-control snapped. Instinctively I arched my hips and cried out as lashes of pleasure thrashed me.

I went manic, gyrating my hips, thrusting two fingers into my vagina and soared toward ecstasy. Convulsions gripped me and I gasped as I rode the deep, penetrating contractions.

I cried out as my release overwhelmed me and spun me into the wonderous world of pleasure I craved so much since Chad had introduced me to it.

My vagina spasmed and my ass tightened as the driving pleasure roared through me. It was never ending and I loved sailing within the spasms. Finally the shudders ebbed, and I lay on the beach panting, my naked body dotted with perspiration.

I longed to reach out and slip into my bikini top and bottom, but I ignored the impulse. I simply wanted to languish here in the aftereffects of my orgasm, enjoying the brisk, hot wind as it kissed every part of my exposed flesh.

Lying here, fully exposed, was heaven and pure peace.

I listened to the crying seagulls as they sailed overhead and heard the pounding surf roar onto the beach mere feet away. The nature sounds were my lullaby. An ocean song of freedom that lulled me to sleep.

I dreamed of nothing. Didn't want to. This was my special time away from everything.

No coach. No grandma. No two-timing ex-boyfriend who hadn't even thought that *maybe* I might want to be invited into that first-aid shack with him and another lifeguard.

No, nothing.

It was nice, black, and calm. I slept deep. Really deep, loving the relaxation and I didn't come awake until I heard the ominous rumble of thunder as it echoed all around me with a warning force.

Oh, crap!

I opened my eyes and stared up into the sky. No longer was it a happy clear brilliant baby blue, but now there were low hanging gun-metal gray-colored billows gazing down at me. I gasped as silver lightning forked out of the rolling clouds and into the nearby ocean.

Adrenaline seared through me as I scrutinised the area where I'd left my towel, sandals and car keys.

Dread hollowed out my tummy. I couldn't see the coastline beneath the silvery sheets of rain that were speeding toward me. For a split second, I thought about hunkering down here and waiting out the storm, but there was no overhang on the lighthouse to protect me from the rain.

Panic snapped through me and I quickly donned my bikini. Then, without hesitation, I dove into the water.

Immediately, I realized I was in trouble. The wind had picked up big time while I'd languished and the waves were powerfully rough as they curled over me with ominous force. Despite my nap, it appeared I wasn't as refreshed as I should have been, but hell, I wasn't going to spend the night out here.

Besides, Grandma would freak out having her slave gone missing!

My mouth went dry with fear as the tumultuous waves literally picked me up and rolled me up and toward the sea.

Oh man! Come on! Give me a break!

I forced every ounce of my energy into fighting the waves. I just needed to swim to the shoreline, then I could walk back to my car.

Desperation gripped me as another wave curled over me like a giant arm. I held my breath as it pulled me under. Terror made me kick my feet and swim like a mad woman until my head burst through the choppy surface.

I dragged in a deep breath, inhaling the rain-streaked salty air.

Shit! That was close!

Thunder crashed overhead and bright flashes of lightning reassured me I was still alive.

But for how long?

I pushed my fear and despair from my mind. Forced myself to concentrate with my entire being into doing what needed doing, which was staying alive and swimming back to shore.

I didn't know how long I swam. Didn't even know I was going the right way, but my arms began cramping and my legs felt floppy. I kept sinking into the quietness beneath the ocean and every time I managed to break to the surface, the roar of the waves and crackles of thunder made me think about going back under where it was quiet.

Water kept smashing against my face and it was getting harder to breathe. My eyes burned from the salt water and I could barely see.

Slowly my thoughts turned to giving up.

Just give up, Katie. Open your mouth and let the water in. Just go limp. It'll be over soon.

Just then something hard and orange nudged against my shoulder. I heard a shout. A man yelling to grab hold to the life preserver.

Huh? I must be hallucinating. I could only see the big waves crashing into my face. Another black wave rolled over me. I swallowed salt water. Coughed. Swallowed more.

Shit!

I was going to give up. I had no choice.

Another giant wave curled over me and swallowed me. I just held my breath and went under. I became limp. All my fight was gone. It was time to die.

I envisioned myself as a ragdoll just flopping around in the sea. I couldn't hold my breath anymore, and for a second I was terrified as the water seeped into me.

This is it. I'm dead.

Then suddenly, I felt very calm as the breath was sucked out of me.

So calm.

Everything went black.

Chapter Three

"She's coming around," I heard a man's voice echo in my ears as I puked up the bitter salty water I'd inhaled and swallowed.

Man, I felt bad. My throat was on fire and my nostrils burned. And I was terribly cold. I couldn't stop shivering. My teeth were chattering a mile a minute too.

"She's hypothermic. We need to get her to the shack and out of that bikini and slowly warm her up," a familiar man's voice replied.

I recognized it instantly.

Oh crap. My ex-boyfriend, Chad.

I felt myself being lifted and then carried. Rain pelted my cold face, but I didn't care. For awhile I just listened to the roar of the surf, the crash of the thunder and then it suddenly got quieter. A moment later I was being lowered onto something soft.

I opened my eyes. They burned because of the salt water I'd been in, but I could see him clearly and my tummy somersaulted in a nice kind of way. He looked so hot in the way he gazed at me with such concern in his brown eyes.

Why in the world had I broke up with him again? My mind whirled with that question as I stared at him and appraised his features.

His medium-length sandy brown hair was wet and slicked back off his face just as always. I'd admired the fact that all he had to do was smooth a hand over his hair and push it back off his forehead and it would stay that way.

He was nicely tanned from the sun and he was broad shouldered with slim hips. He wore my favorite black Speedo bathing suit which illuminated the outline of his large shaft.

I could hear scissors snipping and I looked to my right to see Chad was cutting one bikini strap and then the other one. I felt my ice-cold skimpy top being removed, exposing my chilled breasts to him.

"Nice breasts," I heard a man say.

Surprisingly, my cheeks warmed at his compliment.

"Shut up, Stretch. That's unprofessional and she's awake," Chad replied tartly.

"Get off her bottoms too," came Stretch's voice.

As far as I could tell, there were just the two of them in the small building. From the several life preservers hanging on a nearby wall and several metal shelves filled with first aid stuff, I figured I was in the lifeguards' first aid shack. This was the shack the men took the flirty surfer girls to. The same shack I'd seen Chad and another lifeguard coming out of with one of those chicks.

And here I had almost drowned to get the luxury of seeing inside this building.

I heard the scissors snipping and felt my bottoms being removed.

Then a fluffy blanket covered me. But I still felt awfully cold.

"When is this storm going to let up?" I heard Stretch murmur. He'd moved to the lone window and was gazing out. Rivulets of rain ran down the glass and it was pretty dark outside.

"Anyone out there?" Chad asked as he placed two hot fingers to my wrist. He was checking my pulse.

"There're only three cars left. Yours, mine and Katie's. But we can't get out though."

"Why not?" Chad's head snapped up and he frowned at Stretch.

"Because I can see from here the road is washed away and there's a river running right through it. The landline is out and my cell phone doesn't work, so unless yours is working, she's our patient now."

"I left mine at home this morning. Forgot to charge it last night and was in too much of a hurry to look for the charger and bring it with me."

"Yeah, great. Well it's her fault we're still here," Stretch complained.

Chad shook his head and rolled his eyes.

"Had you not been watching her masturbating through your damn high-tech binoculars, like you always do, I'd be home making supper."

Oh my goodness! Chad had been watching me?

I should be embarrassed, but surprisingly I wasn't. Maybe the hypothermia was making me not care?

I noticed his cheeks redden and I couldn't help but let out a little giggle. He'd made fun of my red cheeks and now he was blushing himself!

"Yeah, and had I not been watching her, she'd be dead now, wouldn't she?" Chad snapped. Anger laced his voice and I was glad he was sticking up for me.

"How are you feeling??" Chad asked as he caught me watching him.

"Still c-c-old. Ice-c-c-old." I replied through chattering teeth.

"Don't we have any more emergency blankets?" Chad growled.

"You're the one who orders stuff and you were on vacation. I told you, before you left we needed some because someone broke in and stole the few we had left."

Chad inhaled deeply as if trying to calm himself.

"They were ordered and should have been here by now," he said in a tight voice.

Stretch moved away from the window and came closer. I caught him watching me.

"Do you have any blankets or clothes in your car, Katie?" Stretch asked.

I shook my head.

"I d-don't like being this c-cold," I complained.

A tinge of panic rippled through me. What if I never got warm again? I couldn't live like this!

Chad nodded, and he was biting on his lower lip. I knew he was thinking. Formulating a plan. He always worried his bottom lip when he was planning something.

"The only alternative is sandwiching her between us. Use our body heat to warm her," Chad said in a hoarse voice.

Stretch made a strangled laugh.

"A manwich? With your ex?"

"Come on. Let's be quick. She needs to get warmed up. You'll have to lose your wet swimsuit."

Stretch cursed and shook his head.

I frowned, wondering what his problem might be.

"Come on, man. You know how I am around naked ladies," Stretch complained.

"She's seen an erection before. Just control yourself." Chad said.

I smiled. At least I think I did. I watched Chad strip off his tight bathing suit. My eyes widened and my cold pussy shivered with a spark of heat as I saw his giant penis.

Oh my goodness, I remembered his cock quite well. From the two-inch wide girth that fit me so well, to the thick blue veins that interlaced the entire velvet-encased eight-inch hard length that held his scrumptious purplish mushroom-shaped cockhead.

Awareness began to melt that godawful cold that was clinging to me like a bad virus. Chad stood beside me where I lay on a sheet-covered mattress which made me wonder why they hadn't covered me with the sheet.

Heck, if the blanket wasn't warming me, then I figure the sheet wouldn't do the job either. Movement caught my gaze from my left side and I turned my head to watch Stretch lowering his tight bathing suit.

I held my breath as his giant serpent of a cock uncurled and stuck straight out like a steel pole and it was flushed red with excitement.

Obviously seeing my naked breasts moments earlier had turned him on.

Big time. `

Stretch's cock was a bit shorter than Chad's but much thicker. And I detected a glisten of pre-cum at the tip of his plum-shaped cockhead. Now I understood his complaint. It appeared he got quite aroused on seeing a naked woman, even one who'd almost died.

But hey, I could forgive him for his arousal. I must be an attractive woman. Until now, I hadn't really thought of myself in that way.

Both men were extraordinarily well-endowed and something naughty and hot quivered deep inside my lower belly at the sight of two juicy shafts.

I liked this heat. Wanted to explore it. Needed more of it.

Suddenly I knew if I could claim this passion burning deep inside of me, then I would be able to kill off my good-girl innocence and truly embrace my true self. My brush with death would turn me into a woman who wanted to expose herself to all things sexual.

I could feel my heart begin to beat faster as Chad lifted the blanket. The mattress moved as he slid his hot body in beside me.

"Come on. Turn on your side toward me. This will work better if we snuggle nice and close like we used to," Chad said. His voice sounded thick and hoarse.

Geez. I had to be practically dead before the man decided to pay attention to me again.

I nodded and bit back a sudden swell of emotions as I remembered the two of us in his tiny apartment, lying on his sofa bed, snuggled in each other's arms with barely enough room for us on the mattress.

Just like now.

I scooted close to him and heard him exhale as our bodies touched. His face was mere inches from my face and I relished the warm air of his breath caressing my cheeks. His hot legs pushed against mine and his boiling chest pressed against my breasts, but he kept his lower half from touching me. Despite that, I enjoyed his body heat wafting between the few inches separating our bodies.

"You're like an iceberg," Chad said.

"Feel like one too," I admitted.

My, oh, my, he was so nice and warm. I resisted the impulse to reach out and wrap my arms around his waist.

Chad looked over my shoulder.

"Come on, Stretch. Get your ass over here."

"Coming," he grumbled behind me.

Awareness of having a strange man seeing me naked made me tense as the blanket lifted behind me. The mattress moved as Stretch climbed in. He pushed his hot body against mine, lining up his legs against the back of mine, his upper torso against my back and I softly inhaled as the outline of his scorching shaft pressed against the curve of my upper ass cheek.

Chapter Four

"Nice and toasty," I whispered as Stretch's body heat slammed into me.

I could hear the men's breaths quickening. Could feel Stretch's shaft growing larger. I could also feel my ass clenching as I imagined Stretch sliding his cock into me there.

I swallowed as my body tensed.

Chad had closed his eyes, and for several minutes I thought he might have fallen asleep, until he spoke.

"I noticed you aren't trembling as much. Are you feeling better?" he asked.

He'd opened his eyes and his brown gaze was hooded and filled with lust.

"Much better, but still pretty cold," I complained. I didn't want them to move away. I enjoyed feeling two strong male bodies pressed in around me like a *manwich*, using the term Stretch had mentioned earlier.

Chad nodded and fell silent.

Rain pounded against the roof of the shack and flashes of lightning flickered at the lone window. Thunder boomed. It appeared the storm wasn't going anywhere. Neither was the hot need brewing inside of me.

"There is an ancient saying that when you save someone's life, you own them," Stretch murmured. His face touched the back of my head and I could feel his hot breath against my neck. I liked the warmth and the feel of their flesh upon mine.

"Quiet, Stretch. Let her recuperate," Chad broke in.

Stretch had hit on something. I would be dead if they hadn't rescued me. I would be that limp rag doll I had imagined being tossed around out there in the waves. I would be dead meat. Shark food. And I would not even have experienced life.

Or lived my sexual fantasies.

And I wanted to live one of them. Having sex with my ex and with another man at the same time.

And I wanted to do it right now.

I shivered as a cold wave of dread overwhelmed me.

Oh, man, suddenly it felt like life was way too short for everything that I wanted to do, sexually.

"Are you okay?" Chad asked.

I opened my eyes. He was still staring at me and my pussy trembled as I decided on something.

"I-I think. There is a way for you b-both to make me feel really h-hot," I whispered.

Chad grinned. "Oh yeah? What's that? If you want some hot chocolate, the power is out, so I can't boil you up some."

Silly man. Hot chocolate was for kids. And what part of *both of them* didn't he get?

"Make love to me," I said.

Oh, my goodness! Had I said that out loud?

In the enjoyable manner that Stretch tensed against me and the stunned way Chad was staring at me made me realize that yes, I had said my request out loud.

From behind me, Stretch cursed softly beneath his breath.

Chad appeared to recover quickly, his facial expression going stoic.

"That certainly would warm you up, but with hypothermia your core needs to be warmed slowly or you could go into cardiac arrest or organ failure," Chad explained.

Seriously? I was wanting sex and he was offering me an explanation as to why not?

Frustration grabbed a hold of me. Perhaps this man was way too serious for me. Maybe I had been all wrong about him having future written all over him? Did I really need to spell it out to him?

"So, be inventive. Warm me up slowly. Both of you."

Against my ear, Stretch cursed again.

Chad's Adams apple bobbed in his throat as he stared at me.

"You're under duress. You're not thinking clearly. It's unprofessional." Chad murmured.

"I've never thought more clearly. I want to know what those surfer girls experience when they come into this shack."

"You heard the lady," Stretch said with a chuckle.

I didn't push him away as his hot hand slid over my shoulder and he cupped my left breast. His palm scorched my cold flesh. I gasped as he began pinching my nipple. At first it felt painful, foreign. But then my nipple responded.

It elongated, felt bigger. Pleasure mingled with sultry pain.

A nice feeling erupted between my thighs. I felt wet and hot down there as my pussy lips engorged and warm cream seeped down my vagina.

Stretch's movements made the blanket lower and Chad's eyes grew wider as he watched what Stretch was doing to me.

"Katie..." Chad hissed. His voice sounded strangled, unsure.

"Shh, I know what I want. Kiss me. Kiss me all over," I demanded.

I trembled with excitement.

Doubt flooded his eyes. Nice, sexy brown eyes. I'd never gotten enough of looking into them.

"Pretend I'm one of those girls," I whispered.

I wanted this. Yet he hesitated. I could imagine what he was thinking. Screw her brains out so she'll live or keep her as a manwich filling until they could get out of here and make her suffer the cold that was still invading her body.

"No strings," I added for incentive.

"I've got condoms and lube right here in the drawer," Stretch murmured against my neck.

I nodded.

"Get them," I instructed. My voice sounded bold, determined. Aroused.

Stretch's hand slid off my breast and he turned away but didn't get out of bed. A second later, I heard a drawer slide open.

"She's a virgin back there," Chad protested.

"I'll go easy on her," he said hoarsely.

I could tell Chad was finally getting enthusiastic in the way his nostrils flared as he looked at me like a predator about to get something he wanted.

A rip of foil snapped through the air. I could hear Stretch sliding on a condom and then the slurp of lube. Juicy sounds ripped through the air as he massaged the lube onto his cock.

"Reach back and take me inside of you," Stretch growled as he once again stretched out behind me.

I bit my bottom lip and did as he asked.

I moved my arm back and down and quickly felt his swollen shaft throbbing against my palm.

I wrapped my fingers around his solid, pulsing flesh and angled it toward my ass.

I gasped at the awesome feel of his smooth plum-shaped cockhead as I pressed it against the tight circle of muscles and nerves around my anal opening.

STRETCH HISSED AND I trembled and gasped as I pushed the tip of his scorching cockhead into me.

He was big and swollen and my anal canal felt so tight and protested the invasion by clenching around him.

"That's it, Katie. We'll do this nice and slow," Stretch murmured against my ear.

His arm slid over my shoulder once more and he cupped my breast with his palm. His strong fingers tweaked and pulled my nipples until my pussy and ass tightened with naughty need.

"Your turn," I whispered to Chad who had been watching my reaction at having another man's penis pushing into my behind.

"Are you sure you want this?" Chad asked. His eyes blazed with heat and I found myself responding.

I nodded jerkily.

At the moment there was nothing more that I wanted. Especially figuring I should be dead.

"We do this slow. So her core warms slowly. Got it?" Chad said as he looked over my shoulder and appeared to hold Stretch's gaze with warning.

"I know how to warm up a woman nice and slow, my man. I wasn't born yesterday."

Chad nodded and I shuddered as his hand settled on my hip. His calloused fingers began to knead my cold flesh there.

He drew his face closer to me, his warm breath caressing my chilled cheeks. Then his hot mouth melted over my trembling lips in a soft, heated kiss. I moaned my appreciation as pleasure whipped through me and he deepened the kiss.

The sound of my moan must have turned Stretch on even more as his cock nudged into me another inch. His partially buried, lubed shaft felt oh-so-big and I closed my eyes against the burst of pleasure pain as his hard flesh throbbed inside me.

Thankfully, he didn't move deeper. He must have sensed I needed time to get used to his penetration.

Chad's mouth became more forceful capturing my attention. His teeth nipped at my lower lip, creating pinpricks of seductive pain. And then he licked my bruised flesh, soothing the fire he'd created. He slipped his tongue past my lips and boldly pushed into my mouth to duel with my tongue.

The impact made me heady.

Chad's hand slipped beneath my other breast. He began massaging me there as he drew me deeper into his kiss, then he pinched and pulled on my nipple much in the same way Stretch continued to do at my other breast.

I sank into the pleasure both men created. The icy grip claiming my core released and thankfully I began to warm.

I welcomed the hotness. Oh, how I welcomed it.

Boldly, I pulled on Stretch's solid penis, encouraging him to penetrate me deeper. I wanted his heat searing into me, claiming me, possessing me.

I gasped into Chad's mouth as Stretch pushed his cock in another inch.

Hot fire penetrated my ass and my anal muscles protested and clamped tight around his flesh. The pressure was intense and I wasn't sure if I could go on but Stretch breathed softly against my ear and sucked on my earlobe creating an uncontrollable trembling in my shoulders and an erotic clenching of my vagina.

With my free hand, I found Chad's erection. His hot flesh pulsed and jerked as I wrapped my palm and fingers around the thick base and held his throbbing shaft.

In response, Chad's tongue shot into my mouth like a heat seeking missile, making my hands automatically tighten around both of the men's rock-hard throbbing flesh.

Stretch's lips let go of my ear lobe and slowly he slid his mouth along the back of my neck, pressing delicate kisses that had me arching, which made his penis plunge even deeper.

I yelped at the pleasure pain as the pressure became so intense and so blistering hot, I was moaning and writhing between the two lifeguards.

Chad broke the kiss and his face moved lower, his lips kissing my chin and then butterfly kisses along my neck that had me shuddering. I watched as he nudged Stretch's hand from my breast and then Chad's hot lips greedily circled my nipple. He began to suck, drawing on my throbbing bud like a man possessed.

Fire raged through my core as male hands seductively massaged along the curve of my hip and along my abdomen. I loved how their touches chased away the icy cold, leaving me feeling almost normal again.

Well, normal isn't the right word. Feverish with desire. Needy. Desperate for a more intimate contact. Urgent to have the fire of both men's cocks buried deep inside of me.

"I need more. Give me more," I pleaded.

I felt Stretch's hand curl over my shoulder and he gently squeezed.

"Consider me your personal butt plug, beauty. Now trust me on what happens next and stay relaxed," he whispered against my neck.

I didn't know what he meant until he suddenly rolled me halfway on top of him and I cried out as his shaft pierced deeper. Bites of pleasure pain seared into me and the pressure grew so intense I thought for sure Stretch was going to split my behind in two!

Chapter Five

The foreign feeling of heaviness eased and the panic of his fullness had me frantically gasping for breaths. That he was now buried deep inside me had me closing my eyes and willing myself to remain calm as my anal muscles happily spasmed around his sizzling flesh.

"I love the way your ass makes love to my cock," Stretch breathed as he nibbled on my earlobe.

Instinctively I turned my head making him let go of my earlobe and I caught his lips in a kiss. He groaned and kissed me back, his mouth branding my senses and sending shockwaves of pleasure through me.

Suddenly I was riding a wave of high. I wanted to lose myself in a frenzy of pleasure.

As I frantically kissed him I could feel his long, thick shaft vibrating inside me. It was thickening and elongating, stretching deeper. Somewhere in the back of my mind I wondered if that's why they called him Stretch, because he certainly was stretching into my ass.

Now I realized why he'd moved me into this new pose. I was literally impaled on his cock, unable to escape, not that I wanted to, but with this new position I was also fully frontally exposed for Chad.

Chad had easier access to me and he was certainly entertaining himself with my breasts.

His hands were massaging my mounds and he was licking and sucking on one nipple until it was a throbbing mass before he moved his mouth to my other nipple. He pleasured me alternately with his tongue and his teeth, lapping and nipping until my nipple was so hot I could hardly stand the splintering mix of pleasure and pain.

Blindly, I found and then slid my hands upon his muscular chest and was about to push him away because his mouth was becoming so intense, but before I could, he let go of my tender nipple with a loud pop.

His head went lower. My hands fell off his chest and I curled my fingers against the back of his neck.

As Stretch's kiss deepened, I became intoxicated with desire. A hunger for more intimacy was bursting inside me.

Chad's lips moved over my quivering abdomen in mind destroying kisses that had me automatically lifting my left leg. Quickly, I settled it over his muscular shoulder, giving him full access to the intimate zone between my thighs.

As Chad's mouth drew closer to my pussy, I broke the kiss with Stretch and watched Chad with anticipation. During our short time together in our relationship, I had never allowed him to do oral. Had never allowed him to so much as look at my pussy, even when we'd been having sex.

Blame it on my good girl upbringing, But now, I craved him.

I tensed as his face lowered between my thighs.

I whimpered as I waited, filled with awe as his breath caressed my pussy lips. I tried to pull his head forward, but he was like iron. Steadfast.

"Easy Katie, let me look at your pussy," he breathed.

I watched his face. It was lit up with appreciation, a wonderous smile on his mouth. Even his brown eyes glittered with gratitude.

"So damn beautiful. So perfect. Never be afraid of showing a man or a woman your succulent pussy, Katie. Now that I've seen it, I don't think I will ever have enough of looking at it," he whispered.

I was stunned at his words and realized I would never have heard them had I drowned. Something inside of me shifted. My deep-down inner shyness completely disintegrated, replaced with a feeling of daring, and an emotion of wanting to be naughty.

Never again would I be ashamed of my intimate body parts. Screw grandma and her old-fashioned restraints.

The intoxicating way Chad was looking at the apex of my thighs, exhilarated me and I wanted my sexual freedom. I wanted to be just like those surfer girls I envied!

Chad lowered his head and I moaned as his lips tenderly sucked on my labia lips.

A savage need was building in me with lightning speed. My abdominal muscles were tightening and I cried out as Chad lapped luxuriously at my ultra-sensitive clitoris. His tongue was like a whip-master, lashing back and forth, up and down, around and around, until my clit was fever hot and so sensitive that I knew I would climax at any second.

My thighs felt rock-hard and my ass muscles were wrapped ultra-tight around Stretch's big cock.

Every muscle in my body was primed, every nerve ending igniting, sparking, fighting for release. I was aching, and in a really good way.

Stretch was groaning beneath me and Chad was moaning as he continued to play with my clit drawing me closer and closer to the edge of bliss.

Prickling heat and perspiration skipped across my skin with his every tongue lash.

When I thought I could no longer stand the intense tension coursing through my entire body and the throbbing heat growing deep inside my empty vagina, Chad's magical mouth seared over my pussy in one hot fusion.

I exploded!

I cried out Chad's name as the spasms ripped through me in a tsunami of pleasure.

Stretch grabbed my chin and turned my head and then his warm lips melted over mine, cutting off my cries. He kissed me hard and I kept convulsing within the hot shudders that were ripping me apart.

Instinctively I gyrated my hips and fought against Chad's hands on my inner thighs as he held me apart so he could mouth fuck me into oblivion.

He sucked hard and then he slipped his tongue into me, thrusting like a little cock and then withdrawing, licking, and lapping until I was panting and bucking, convulsing with every pleasure hit.

And then Stretch ripped his mouth away at the same time Chad's lips left my body. I felt Stretch moving me until I was entirely upon his body.

I could barely register what was going on as I kept bucking and writhing. The spasms were controlling me and I could barely keep my eyes open as I watched Chad rise up.

In a quick move, he reached out and grabbed a condom from Stretch who was huffing and puffing beneath me. His every breath made his cock tremble in my ass, creating even more spasms. My body flared with heat and I loved it.

In seconds, Chad sheathed himself and then he was moving his muscular body over me.

He lowered himself and I cried out as his mouth melted over mine, then his hard chest flattened my breasts and his thick, juicy penis plunged into my spasming vagina in one solid thrust.

With two cocks buried inside me, I exploded even harder!

Chad withdrew and thrust into me again.

His strokes were persistent and never ending as my vaginal muscles clamped around him and tried to hold him inside. But he was stronger, his cock driving pleasure throughout my entire body.

The sounds of male groans intermingled with my cries of arousal. Shudders raged through me. It was never ending and I loved it!

As the insane spasms began to ebb, Stretch's body tightened and he convulsed beneath me as he orgasmed. Soon after, Chad joined him.

Afterwards, I fell asleep between the two men. Their body heat was so welcome and I much preferred this heat to that horrific icy cold that my two lifeguards had thankfully chased out of me.

Yes, I owed both of them my life and their gratitude for giving me a new outlook on sex.

Sometime during the night, the storm ceased and when morning dawned, I discovered that Chad had rolled off me. I gazed around and found him standing at the lone window of the first aid shack.

Slowly, I managed to untangle myself from Stretch. His cock was still buried inside my ass and he was fast asleep and snoring softly. He seemed oblivious when I managed to climb off him, his cock leaving me with a succulent pop.

I was pleasantly tender in both openings from the sex, but I knew I could get used to this kind of soreness.

I joined Chad at the window and I was surprised when he reached out and slipped his arm around my waist, pulling me up against his hard, muscular body.

"I'd kiss you good morning, Katie, but I've got morning breath," he whispered. A sweet smile brightened his face.

I grinned and he nodded out the window.

"The landline is working. I've already called for assistance. In the meantime, take a look at what you've been missing all these years without seeing a bunch of sunrises."

My breath caught as I gazed out.

Warm hues of purple, bright orange and baby blue colors splashed across the sky and reflected in the quiet glass-like ocean.

"It's so beautiful," I whispered.

Chad hugged me closer.

"So are you."

"Oh, wow. Such a nice compliment. Thank you," I replied.

My body was humming at his words and I wondered how he would respond with what I was about to ask him.

"I had a spectacular night with the two of you. Would you be up for doing it again?"

I held my breath and studied his face as I waited for his answer. He looked serious and was biting his bottom lip.

Such an endearing gesture.

"Katie, I would be willing to do anything to please you. From here on out, would you be my girl again?"

"As long as I am your *only* girl," I replied honestly.

I hoped my jealousy wouldn't ruin it this time around, but I would set boundaries so he knew I wanted to be his one and only.

"And I will be available to you in the sexual department any time you want. I'll continue coming here every day to swim but not to train for the Olympics anymore and when you get the urge to share, I want to be that woman in the manwich. Deal?"

Chad nodded.

"As I said earlier, Katie. I will do anything to please you and if that means you want to be sexually adventurous then I am all in. Deal."

His brown eyes glittered with happiness and I suddenly realized that Chad *was* the man with future written all over him. *The* man for me.

I couldn't have asked for a better guy.

The End

Spunky Girl Publishing Catalog

Jasmine Black
~Erotica~Without the Romance

Here are some more Jasmine Black eBooks...

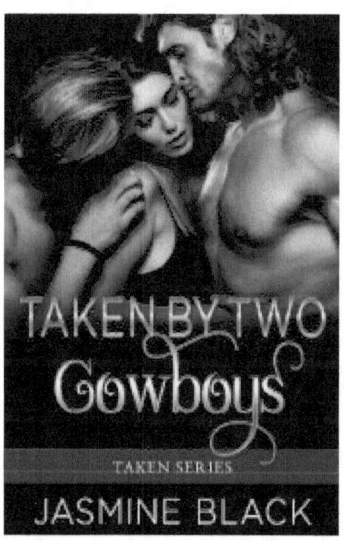

Taken by Two Cowboys

Sierra Allan works hard at her late-father's horse ranch. When her step-brother adds her handy girl services to a private auction to help raise money for the failing ranch, she figures there's no harm...but she's stunned when her services are sold to two sexy cowboys who give her an erotic way to save the ranch—submitting to their dark desires..

Taken by Three Billionaires

Billionaire friends, Liam, Theo and Elijah have just won Princess Isabella in a billionaire card game. Isabella knows exactly what the three men will want from her...she just hadn't expected to have all three of them at once!

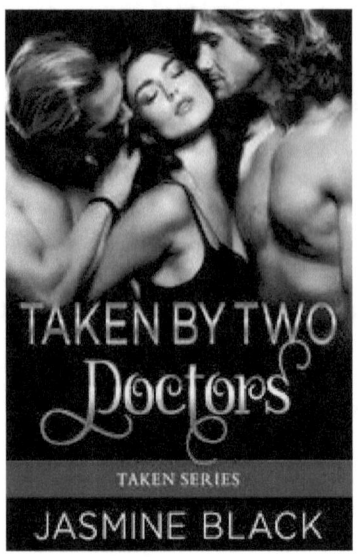

Taken by Two Doctors
A BDSM Medical Fetish Erotica Quickie MFM

Waitress Jean Spelling visits her controversial doctor once a month for some much-needed...stress relief. She looks forward to putting her feet up in the stirrups and enjoys Dr. Ball's naughty unconventional treatments. This time when she arrives, she's surprised to discover that she'll be physically examined by two doctors and they'll prescribe her some much-needed release right there on the examination table!

eBooks in Jasmine Black's Ménage series

Taken by Three Bodyguards
Taken by Three Bikers
Taken by Three Billionaires
Taken by Three Doctors
Taken by Three Cowboys

eBooks in Jasmine Black's Taken series

Taken by Two Prison Guards
Taken by Two Elves
Taken by Two Mountain Men
Taken by Two Cops
Taken by Two Santas
Taken by Two Lifeguards
Taken by Two Firefighters
Taken by Two Bikers
Taken by Two Billionaires
Taken by Two Bosses
Taken by Two Cowboys
Taken by Two Personal Trainers
Taken by Two Carpenters

Jasmine Black Website ~ http://www.jasmine-black.com
Twitter ~ @blackerotica1

Jan Springer ~ Erotic Romance ~

Cowboys For Christmas
Cowboys Online 1 ~ Moose Ranch
Jan Springer
A Canadian Contemporary Ménage Romance m/f/m/m Series

Jennifer Jane (JJ) Watson has spent the past ten Christmases in a maximum-security prison.

The last thing she expects is to get early parole, along with a job on a remote Canadian cattle ranch serving Christmas holiday dinners to three of the sexiest cowboys she's ever met!

Rafe, Brady and Dan thought they were getting a couple of male ex-cons to help out around their secluded ranch, but instead they get an attractive and very appealing female.

In the snowbound wilds of Northern Ontario, female companionship is rare.

It's a good thing the three men like to share...

They're dominating, sexy-as-sin and they fill JJ with the hottest ménage fantasies she's ever had. Suddenly she's craving cowboys for Christmas and wishing for something she knows she can never have...a happily ever after.

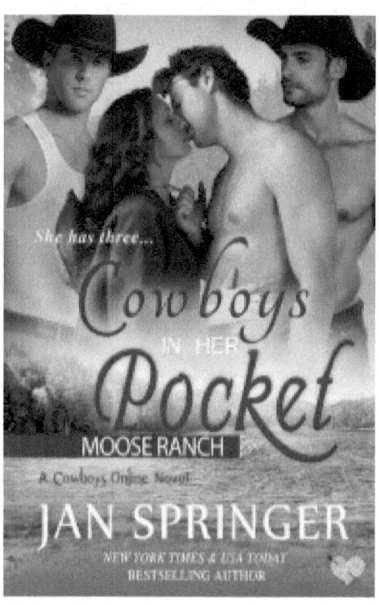

Cowboys In Her Pocket
Cowboys Online 2 ~ Moose Ranch
Jan Springer

*After spending ten years in a maximum-security prison Jennifer Jane (JJ)
Watson got early parole and a job on a remote Canadian cattle ranch
playing housekeeper to three of the sexiest cowboys she's ever met...*

Spring has finally arrived at Moose Ranch, and a single woman fresh out
of prison shouldn't be experiencing scorching ménages with her three
sexy-as-sin cowboys. But JJ's love for her men continues to grow as she
gives into the fevered heat and scorching passions she feels for each of
them.

Life is perfect.

Until her new life is tested when mysterious happenings occur on the
ranch and then one of her cowboys is viciously attacked and injured.

Will JJ's newfound freedom and happiness be ripped away?

Rafe, Brady and Dan never expected to find an attractive and very appealing female to help them out at their secluded ranch. But in the wilds of Northern Ontario, female companionship is rare. It's a good thing the three men like to share...

Brady, Dan and Rafe have never been happier. Their cattle ranch is flourishing and their continued desire to share the sexy woman who cares for them makes their life complete. Until danger threatens to rip everything apart...

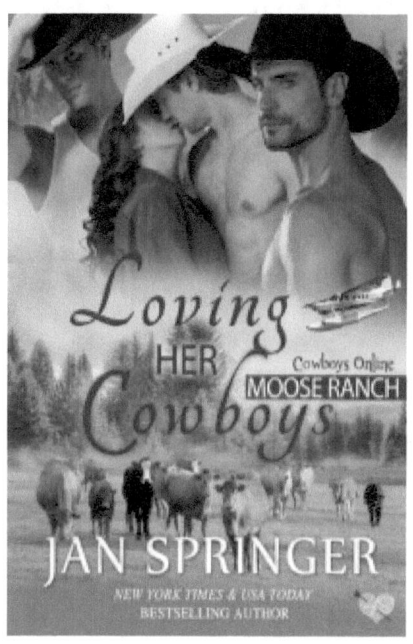

Loving Her Cowboys
Cowboys Online 3 ~ Moose Ranch
Jan Springer

AFTER SPENDING TEN years in a maximum-security prison Jennifer Jane (JJ) Watson got early parole and a job on a remote Canadian cattle ranch playing housekeeper to three of the sexiest cowboys she's ever met...

Her love for her cowboys continues to grow as she gives into fevered heat. But JJ's simmering restlessness explodes and she's seriously making up for lost time by pursuing her dreams. There's only one little problem. She hasn't revealed to her bosses what she's been up to while they're away tending to the cattle. She knows when they discover her secret, there will be hell to pay.

Ranchers Rafe, Dan and Brady have found the woman who completes them. She makes their secluded ranch a home-sweet-home. She's vulnerable, sweet and willing to share her bed with all three of them. But when JJ's secret is unwittingly revealed, they're stunned and angry. They figure it's time to dole out some fiery punishment in some mighty naughty ways...

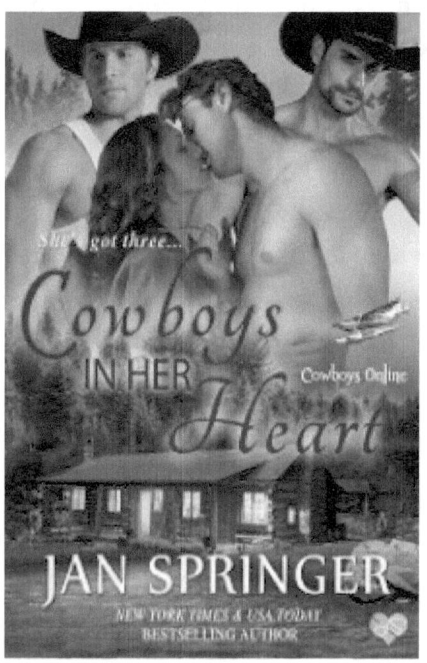

Cowboys In Her Heart
Cowboys Online #4

AFTER SPENDING TEN years in a maximum-security prison, JJ gets unexpected parole and a job on a Canadian ranch serving up scrumptious dinners and lots of hot love to three of the sexiest cowboys she's ever met.

Jennifer Jane "JJ" Watson has never been happier. She's going to have a baby!

Thankfully, their wilderness ranch is a nice distraction for her three sexy cowboys while she's away flying her plane. But when she's home, her dominant hunks are tending to her naughty pregnant cravings and that includes plenty of sizzling ménages.

Rafe, Brady and Dan don't much like the idea of their woman flying the Canadian skies and being at the mercy of the unpredictable Northern Ontario weather. They would prefer having her warming their beds twenty-four seven. But she has a way of getting what she wants and right now she needs her new-found freedom.

Worst fears are realized when JJ, her friend and JJ's plane suddenly go missing and she doesn't come back home to them.

Always Her Cowboys
Cowboys Online 5 ~ Moose Ranch

1

Reader Advisory: Best to read in order. 1. Cowboys for Christmas, 2. Cowboys in Her Pocket, 3. Loving Her Cowboys, 4.Cowboys in Her Heart, 5. Always Her Cowboys. 6. Her Forever Cowboys 7. Claiming Her Cowboys

A Canadian Contemporary Ménage Romance m/f/m/m

JENNIFER JANE (JJ) Watson has spent ten Christmases in a maximum-security prison. The last thing she expected was to get early parole, along with a job on a remote Canadian cattle ranch serving Christmas holiday dinners to three of the sexiest cowboys she's ever met!

Rafe, Brady and Dan thought they were getting male ex-cons to help out around their secluded ranch, but instead they got an attractive and very appealing female. In the snowbound wilds of Northern Ontario, female companionship is rare. It's a good thing the three men like to share...

Christmas is coming once again to Moose Ranch and with JJ's due date approaching, she's distracting herself from anxiety attacks by

---

1. https://janspringerauthor.files.wordpress.com/2017/11/alwayshercowboys_ebook-1new.jpg

keeping herself ultra-busy preparing for the arrival of her baby and planning Moose Ranch's first annual Christmas party!

In having a wee baby on the way, there's a lot of stress for Brady, Rafe and Dan. Especially due to JJ's decision on having a wilderness mid-wife deliver the baby *at their secluded ranch* - with *all* of them present for the birth! But their concerns don't stop the men from showing JJ how much they love her...out of bed and in!

With wicked snowstorms, a grounded bush plane, a cheerful holiday party and a sweet baby on the way, the owners of Moose Ranch know this will be one sparkling Christmas season they won't soon forget...

PLUS: HER FOREVER COWBOYS ~ Snowy Creek Ranch #1 Cowboys Online #6

Claiming Her Cowboys ~ Moose Ranch #6 Cowboys Online #7

Risqué Girl Delights Boxed Set
(Contemporary Erotic Romance)

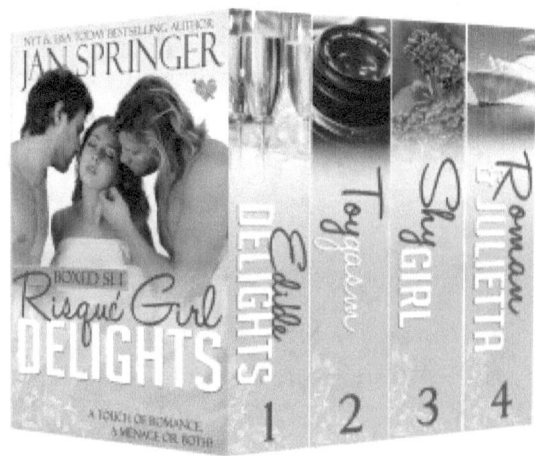

2

...a touch of romance, a ménage or both?

Edible Delights

YEARS AGO ALLIE MASTERS lost herself in the scorching passion of a ménage a trois relationship with her two bosses. In order to regain her independence, she walked away.

Max and Nick were very fulfilled with their gorgeous assistant. The lovemaking was breathtaking and both men willingly shared the woman they wanted to spend the rest of their lives with. Then she left.

Now Max and Nick have decided it's time to seduce Allie back into their lives.

Toygasm

IT'S A CASE OF MISTAKEN identity when the two owners of Sexy Toys, show up for an erotic several day photo shoot of their toys with famous nude model Cammie Creek.

2. https://janspringerauthor.files.wordpress.com/2015/02/rgdelights_box_js_3d_noshadow-1.jpg

Cammie believes the two hunks are the male models she's supposed to work with. Usually she doesn't mix business with pleasure, but when they're seducing her right there in front of the camera, she can't resist turning them into her own personal naughty toys.

Josh and Jode are enjoying the perks of being male models; hot lust, sizzling toys and the best pleasure they've ever had. But how will Cammie react when she discovers they're actually her bosses and not just male models?

Shy Girl

FINALLY FREE OF AN abusive relationship, "Shy Girl" Emma McCall sheds her inhibitions and explores her sensual side at Club Rendezvous, a club specializing in the Alternate Lifestyle.

At the club she's surprised to find Logan Masters, a sexy hunk she's secretly fantasized about since college. With Logan's help, Emma will experience her ultimate fantasy - a scorching ménage a trois.

Roman and Julietta

HER PERFECT LOVER...

Modern day pirate Julietta Black's life has always been immersed in the violent and traditional ways of piracy. When her family's arch enemy puts a hit out on her family, Julietta knows there's only one way to lift the hit; she must kidnap the enemy's sexy grandson and force a union between the two warring families. Night after night, wrapped in Roman's strong arms, she can't deny the searing attraction blazing between them. Nor can she deny he now holds her heart as well as her life in his hands.

His dream angel...

When Roman Prince's mysterious captor offers him a luscious woman to bed, fierce desire ignites, melting his usually tight self-control. Lust quickly turns to love as he enjoys their naughty trysts more than he should. How will he react when he discovers he's been kidnapped, not for a ransom, but captured for his sperm?

Alpha Outlaws Boxed Set (Books 1-5 Outlaw Lovers)
5 Books!!

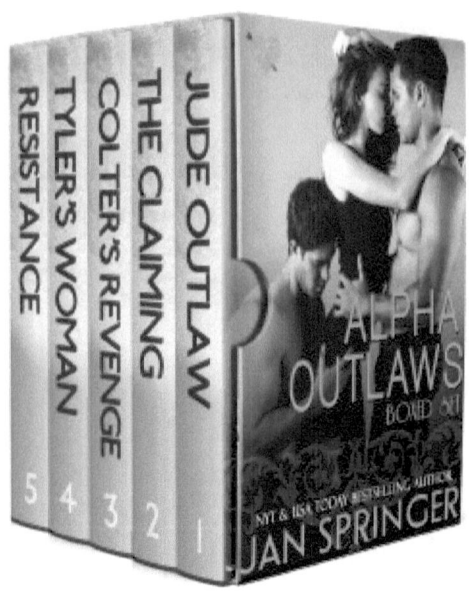

3

IN A WORLD GONE MAD...

A fast-acting virus has killed a majority of the world's female population. With the creation of The Claiming Law, groups of men suddenly have the right to claim a female as their sensual property and the sexy Outlaw brothers are going to declare ownership of the women they love...any way they can.

Jude Outlaw

When Cate Callahan learns Jude is coming home from the Terrorist Wars and is ready to claim her under the new law—with the help of his four brothers—she steals their boat and escapes to the high seas. Unfortunately, her runaway bid for freedom doesn't last long.

Quickly capturing his lover, Jude rekindles the flames and seduces Cate back into his bed.

---

3. https://janspringerauthor.files.wordpress.com/2010/07/alphaoutlaws_js_box_final.jpg

But Jude holds a secret that could make him lose Cate forever...

PLUS

The Claiming

Seeking refuge from the Claiming Law, Callie Callahan hides in a deserted cabin in the Maine woods and is shocked when her ex-flame finds her. She's always craved being in Luke Outlaw's arms. Tasting him. Touching him. Taking him deeply within her. So, what's a girl to do but to delve into the sinful delights he offers.

Luke has finally reunited with the love of his life. He knows there is only one way to keep Callie safe and with him forever. He'll do it with the help of his three brothers and an assortment of naughty toys. Rekindling the flames between them, he unleashes Callie's sensual side, taking her in ways she never dreamed possible, all with the ultimate goal of introducing her to the Outlaw Lovers and The Claiming.

Colter's Revenge

Revenge belongs to Dr. Colter Outlaw when he unexpectedly reunites with the beautiful woman who broke his heart during the Terrorist Wars. Capturing her, collaring her and holding her against her will, he seduces her, fills her with wicked desires and naughty cravings for a delicious ménage. Fully intent on breaking her heart and walking away, Colter's plans unravel when he submits to the carnal pleasures Ashley gives him so freely.

Colter had told her he loved her. He'd whispered promises of rescue from her life as a slave, but when he'd suddenly disappeared, she'd been devastated. Infected with a version of the X-virus that leaves Ashley Blakely sexually excited on a daily basis, she has come to Pleasure Palace to bid on a cure for her illness. She never expected her Outlaw Lover to be there and screw her plans. Nor did she expect to give him her heart and body so easily...

Tyler's Woman

For years Tyler Outlaw and his best friend, Hunter Brown, endured brutal torture and worse in an overseas terrorist prison. Finally, free of their hell, they return home intent on seducing Laurie into their erotic-filled fantasies.

Laurie Callahan has always experienced red-hot pleasure and passionate love in Tyler Outlaw's arms. But when he's pronounced MIA, presumed dead in the Terrorist Wars, Laurie's world is shattered, and her heart is broken.

Shocked to discover Tyler is alive and he's taken a male lover, Laurie is thrust into a sensual world of sizzling seductions, scorching ménages and the carnal desires that both scarred men crave. But she fears Tyler won't want her when he discovers she's not the same woman he left behind...

****READER CAUTION IS ADVISED (m/m forced scenes) ****

Resistance

In the near future, a virus has been unleashed, killing a majority of the world's female population, forcing the introduction of the Claiming Law. A law that states men have all the rights and women are sexual property claimable by groups of men.

Fugitive female...

Renegade Resistance leader Reena "Red" Wilde is in for the fight of her life when she experiences an erotic attraction to the two most dangerous men she's ever met.

Black ops assassin...

Months ago, Will "Blade" Smith spent one sizzling evening in the arms of a red-haired seductress. Now she's his next assignment. One look into her gorgeous eyes and he's wrestling his heated cravings for her all over again.

Bounty Hunter...

When Cade Outlaw nabs his bounty, sexy-as-sin Reena Wilde, his profession dictates she's hands-off. But he can't ignore the magnetic sparks between them...or that she is the biggest temptation of his life.

Resistance is futile...

After Reena escapes Cade and Will and falls prey to a band of evil hunters, she's grateful her sexy hunks come to her rescue...and in return, saves their lives. Trapped in a solitary cabin during a wicked snowstorm, she can't resist her two, well-hung studs, nor can she deny they've claimed her heart.

Many more Jasmine Black and Jan Springer eBooks, print books, audiobooks plus translated eBooks and print books can be found at http://www.janspringer.com and http://www.jasmine-black.com

Here are ways we can connect:

Jasmine Black Website at http://janspringerauthor.wordpress.com/jasmine-black/

Jan Springer Website at http://www.janspringer.com[1]

Instagram – http://www.instagram.com/janspringerauthor

Facebook - https://www.facebook.com/janspringereroticromance

Twitter Jan Springer- https://twitter.com/janspringer @janspringer

Twitter Jasmine Black - https://twitter.com/blackerotica1 @blackerotica1

Pinterest - http://www.pinterest.com/janspringer1/

Jan's Blog - http://janspringerauthor.wordpress.com/blog-2/

Happy Reading,

Jasmine Black / Jan Springer

---

1.   http://www.janspringer.com/

Don't miss out!

Visit the website below and you can sign up to receive emails whenever Jasmine Black publishes a new book. There's no charge and no obligation.

https://books2read.com/r/B-A-GIJD-VJPDC

BOOKS 2 READ

Connecting independent readers to independent writers.